Go, Nan, Go!

and

On the Log

'Go, Nan, Go!' and 'On the Log'
An original concept by Cath Jones
© Cath Jones

Illustrated by Valeria Issa

Published by MAVERICK ARTS PUBLISHING LTD
Studio 3A, City Business Centre, 6 Brighton Road,
Horsham, West Sussex, RH13 5BB
© Maverick Arts Publishing Limited May 2018
+44 (0)1403 256941

A CIP catalogue record for this book is available at the British Library.

ISBN 978-1-84886-343-9

Maverick
www.maverickbooks.co.uk

Pink

This book is rated as: Pink Band (Guided Reading)
This story is decodable at Letters and Sounds Phase 2.

Go, Nan, Go!

and

On the Log

By
Cath Jones

Illustrated by
Valeria Issa

The Letter G

Trace the lower and upper case letter with a finger. Sound out the letter.

Around,
up,
down,
around

Around,
up,
lift,
cross

4

Some words to familiarise:

Nan   hot   sun

High-frequency words:

is   go   the   no   in

Tips for Reading 'Go, Nan, Go!'

- Practise the words listed above before reading the story.

- If the reader struggles with any of the other words, ask them to look for sounds they know in the word. Encourage them to sound out the words and help them read the words if necessary.

- After reading the story, ask the reader who wins the race at the end of the story.

Fun Activity

Have your very own race!

Go, Nan, Go!

Mum is hot in the sun.

Dad is hot in the sun.

Go, Nan, go!

10

Pop is hot in the sun.

Tom is hot in the sun.

Nick is hot in the sun.

Is Nan hot?

No!

The Letter Q

Trace the lower and upper case letter with a finger. Sound out the letter.

*Around,
up,
down,
up*

*Around,
lift,
cross*

Some words to familiarise:

log rat bug

High-frequency words:

the on

Tips for Reading 'On the Log'

- Practise the words listed above before reading the story.

- If the reader struggles with any of the other words, ask them to look for sounds they know in the word. Encourage them to sound out the words and help them read the words if necessary.

- After reading the story, ask the reader what happens when the dog sits on the log.

Fun Activity

Make your own seesaw out of a rock and piece of long cardboard!

On the Log

The bug sat on the log.

The cat sat on the log.

The rat sat on the log.

The bat sat on the log.

The hen sat on the log.

The dog sat on the log!

Book Bands for Guided Reading

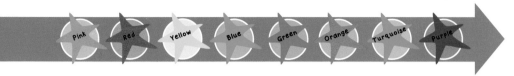

Pink   Red   Yellow   Blue   Green   Orange   Turquoise   Purple

Book Band Pink

Bad Dog and No, Nell, No!	Meg and Rat and Puff! Puff! Puff!	Cool Duck and Lots of Hats	Ned in Bed and Fun at the Park	Peck, Hen, Peck! and Ben's Pet
978-1-84886-287-6	978-1-84886-286-9	978-1-84886-249-4	978-1-84886-285-2	978-1-84886-248-7

Dot and Dan and Snack Attack	Go, Nan, Go! and On the Log	I Can Get It and Hop In!	Tag! and In Pip's Bag	Tug! Tug! and Lots of Spots	
978-1-84886-346-0	978-1-84886-343-9	978-1-84886-345-3	978-1-84886-342-2	978-1-84886-344-6	Plus many more titles in the scheme!

To view the whole Maverick Readers scheme, please visit:

www.maverickbooks.co.uk/early-readers

The Institute of Education book banding system is a scale of colours that reflects the various levels of reading difficulty. The bands are assigned by taking into account the content, the language style, the layout and phonics.

Maverick Early Readers are a bright, attractive range of books covering the pink to purple bands. All of these books have been book banded for guided reading to the industry standard and edited by a leading educational consultant.